Daniel Foot

Poems on Various Occasions

To Which are Added, by Particular Desire, three Letters on Moral Subjects

and Four Speeches...

Daniel Foot

Poems on Various Occasions
To Which are Added, by Particular Desire, three Letters on Moral Subjects and Four Speeches...

ISBN/EAN: 9783744716321

Printed in Europe, USA, Canada, Australia, Japan

Cover: Foto ©Andreas Hilbeck / pixelio.de

More available books at **www.hansebooks.com**

P O E M S

O N

VARIOUS OCCASIONS.

To which are added,

BY PARTICULAR DESIRE,

THREE LETTERS

ON MORAL SUBJECTS,

A N D

FOUR SPEECHES

DELIVERED AT

A LITERARY SOCIETY.

By the late Mr. *D. FOOT.*

Scribimus indocti doctique ———

Hor

CHICHESTER:
Printed by and for W. Andrews, and sold by
G. Robinson, in Pater-noster-Row, London.

M,DCC,LXXVII.

[*Price One Shilling.*]

P R E F A C E.

THE following Poems are presented to the Public, at the Request of many of Mr. Foot's Friends, who admired his Ingenuity, and rever'd his Character. They were written in his Hours of Retirement from more necessary Pursuits, and may be consider'd as the Effusions of a sincere, and grateful Heart, ever ready to distinguish Merit by some literary Mark of Approbation, and Regard. Did a good Man breathe his last, he pour'd forth the mournful Elegy to his Memory. Did any one appear conspicuous for his public Worth, he paid him the just Tribute of honest Applause. Did a deserving Friend survive a dangerous Illness, he was sure to offer the first Congratulations on his Recovery.

It

It was with a View to perpetuate thefe little Specimens of his poetical Skill, that his Father very obligingly confented to their Publication for *the fole Benefit of the Printer*. And it is hop'd, that thofe efpecially who beft knew our Poet's amiable and virtuous Qualities, his difinterefted Friendfhip, his filial Piety, and above all, his awful Senfe, and regular Practice of Religion, will receive thefe Productions with that Candor, which is due to the Memory of their deceas'd Author.

SUBSCRIBERS.

(v)

SUBSCRIBERS.

A.

MR. Richard Aldred, Chichester.
Mifs Alms, Chichester.
Mifs Hannah Alms, Chichester.
Mr. Daniel Auften, Chichester.
Mr. James Auften, Chichester.
Mr. Edward Axford, Chichester.

B.

Mr. Jofeph Baker, Junr. Chichester.
Lieut Ball, of the 17th Regiment.
Mr. Edward Barnard, Chichester.
John Bayly, M. D. Chichester.
Mr. William Begley, Chichester.
Mr. William Bennett, Bofham.
Mr. James Biffin, Chichester.
Mr. John Binfted, Junr. Chichester.
Mifs Lydia Blagden, Chichester.
Rev. Mr. Boifdaune, Chichester, 2 Copies.
Mifs Elizabeth Bonnyface, Eaftagate.
Mifs Maria Booker, Chichester.
Mr. John Bridger, Legnefs.
Mr. James Brine, Chichester.
Mr. Thomas Broadbridge, Halnaker.
Mrs. Buckner, Boxgrove.

C.

Mr. Thomas Cain, Chichester.
Mr. Thomas Capell, Junr. Chichester,
Mr. Jofiah Carter, Chichester,
Mifs Chaldecott, Chichester.
Mr. Stephen Challen, Selfea Ifland,
Mrs. Challen, Appledram.
Mr. William Chatfield, Emfworth.
Mifs Elizabeth Clear, Weftbourn.
Mr. William Clowes, Chichester.
Mr. Samuel Cobby, Chichester, 2 Copies.
Mr. James Cobby, Chichester.
Mr. Thomas Collins, Comedian.
Mr. Thomas Cook, Stanfted.
Mr. George Cook, Weftbourn.
Mr. John Cook, Chichester.
Enfign John Cox, of the 17th Regiment.

Mr. James

D.

Mr. James Davis, Comedian.
Mr. Richard Diggens, Chicheſter.
Mr. John Drake, Chicheſter.
Mr. John Drew, Chicheſter, 2 Copies.

E

Mr. William Edſell, Chicheſter.
Miſs Ann Ewen, Chicheſter.

F

Mr. William Farley, Guildford, 4 Copies.
Mr. James Fathers, Chicheſter.
Mr. Robert Flower, Quarter-Maſter in the 7th, or Queen's
   Regiment of Dragoons.
Mr. Joſeph Foſter, Chicheſter,
William Foſter, Gent. Chicheſter.
William Fowler, Gent. Chicheſter.
Mr. Richard Fuller, Chicheſter.

G.

Mr. James Gates, Chicheſter.
Mr. Thomas Geere, Junr. Chicheſter.
Mr. Robert Gruggin, Chicheſter, 2 Copies.

H.

Mr. William Hall, Emſworth.
Mr. Richard Halſey, Chicheſter.
Mrs. Hargrave, Chicheſter,
Mr. John Harraden, Chicheſter.
——— Harriſon, Chicheſter.
Mr. Joſeph Haſkell, Emſworth.
Mrs. Hay, Chicheſter.
Mr. John Heap, Newport, Iſle of Wight.
Miſs Heron, Boxgrove.
Mr. William Higgins, Chicheſter.
Mr. John Hobby, Chicheſter, 2 Copies.
M. Jonathan Holden, Chicheſter.
Mr. Benjamin Holloway, Emſworth.
Rev. Mr. Harris, Havant.
Mr. Till Hollier, Chicheſter.
Mr. Thomas Hollier, Chicheſter.
Mr. Robert Holt, Chicheſter.
Mr. William Holt, Junr. Chicheſter.
Hr. Richard Horton, Emſworth.
Mr. Henry Horwood, Chicheſter.
Mr. William Howard, Chicheſter.
Mr. Philip Humphry, Chicheſter.

Thomas

I.

Mr. Thomas Ide, Chichester.
Mr. Thomas Ireland, Chichester.

J.

Mr. Thomas Jardine, Chichester.
Mr. Charles Jennings, Chichester.
Miss Jesser, Chichester.
Miss M. Myrtilla Jesser, Chichester.
Mr. Yarrall Johnson, Senr. Chichester.
Mr. William Johnson, Chichester.

K.

Mr. James Knight, Chichester.

L.

Mr. James Lacey, Junr. Chichester.
Miss Lambert, Chichester.
Mr. Thomas Larby, Walberton.
Mr. Joseph Long, Shopwick.
Mr. John Luffe, Chichester.
Mrs. Luxford, Chichester.

M.

Miss Maclene, Hackney.
Mr. Geo. Madgwick, Chichester, 3 Copies.
Mr. Thomas Malton, London.
Miss Ruth Mant, Chichester.
Mr. John Mant, Chichester.
Mr. John Martin, Chichester.
Mr. George Meckett, Chichester.
Mr. Richard Meckett, Chichester.
Mr. William Melchior, Chichester.
Miss Ann Miller, Chichester.
Mr. Jeremiah Miller, Chichester.
Mr. Richard Miller, Junr. Emsworth.
John Monro, Esq; Fellow of St. John's College, Oxon,
  3 Copies.
Mr. William Moorey, Chichester.

N.

Mr. Samuel Neild, Chichester.
Miss Jane Newland, Chichester.
Mr. Richard Newland, Senr. Chichester.
Mr. Thomas Newland, Junr. Slindon.
Mr. John Newman, Chichester.

O.

Mr. George Osborne, Chichester.

Mr. William

P.

Mr. William Palmer, Chichester.
Mr. John Palmer, Petworth.
Mr. John Parvin, Chichester.
Mr. Edward Pasco, Chichester.
Mr. Francis Peat, Chichester.
Miss Peckham, Chichester.
Harry Peckham, Esq; Recorder of Chichester.
John Peerman, Esq; Mayor of Chichester.
Mrs. Pelham, Chichester.
Mr. Oliver Peniket, Boxgrove.
Mr. Petit, Quarter-Master in the 7th, or Queen's, Regiment of Dragoons.
Miss Sally Philpott, Chichester.
Master Richard Phillpott, Chichester.
Mr. Richard Pirce, Comedian.
Mr. William Powell, Chichester.
Barrington Price, Esq; of the 7th Regiment, or Queen's Dragoons.
Mr. John Pryer, Chichester, 2 Copies.

Q.

Mr. Robert Quennell, Junr. Chichester.

R.

Mrs. Sarah Randall, Bersted.
Master Raper, Chichester.
Mr. Willoughby Rhoades, Chichester.
Mr. Daniel Richards, Chichester.
Mr. William Ridge, Chichester.
Miss Jane Rishmond, Chichester.

S.

Thomas Sanden, M. D. Chichester.
Mrs. Elizabeth Sanders, Shopwick.
Mr. Robert Sanders, Chichester.
Mr. Joseph Sanders, Chichester, 2 Copies.
John Shilburn, Esq; Chichester.
Mr. Henry Silverlock, Chichester.
Mr. Daniel Singer, Chichester.
Mr. John Smart, Chichester.
Mrs. Ruth Smith, Chichester.
Mr. Charles Stares, Emsworth.
Mr. Robert Steel, Chichester.
Mr. James St. Clair, Quarter-Master in the 7th or Queen's Regiment of Dragoons.
Miss Mary Stocker, Bersted.

T.

Mr. John Tapner, Boxgrove.

Mr. Richard

Mr. Richard Taylor, Emſworth.
Miſs Thomſon, Chicheſter.
Mr. William Tireman, Chicheſter.
Mr. Thomas Trew, Chicheſter.
Mr. John Tribe, Chicheſter.
Mr. John Tupper, Chicheſter.
Mrs. Sarah Turner, Chicheſter, 2 Copies.
Mr. Thomas Turner, Weſtbourn.

U

Mrs. Upton, Colworth.

W.

Maſter Charles Webber, Chicheſter.
Mr. John Weller, Junr. Chicheſter.
Mr. Richard Weſt, Chicheſter.
Mr. James Weſt, Chicheſter.
Mr. John Weſt, Junr. Chicheſter.
Mr. Thomas White, Chicheſter.
John Williams, Eſq; Chicheſter.
Mr. Samuel Williams, Chicheſter.
Mr. William Woods, Chicheſter.
Miſs Mary Woodman, Fiſhbourn.
Mr. William Wooldridge, Chicheſter.

CONTENTS.

CONTENTS:

Elegy on Mr. George Blagden,   *Page* 1

The 1st Pfalm imitated,   - - - - 3

Epitaph on a Brother and Sister,   - - 5

Verses on the Boarding-School for Young } *ibid.*
   Ladies in Chichester, - - - }

True Excellence, an Ode,   : - - 6

Friendship, a Poem,   - - - - 9

Verses addreffed to Mr. William Farley,   13

To the Rev. Mr. Walker, on hearing him } 14
   preach at Chichester Cathedral April 1775, }

An Hymn of Gratitude,   - - - 16

Ad Amicum,   - - : - - 18

Tranflation thereof,   - - - : 19

The Firft of May, an Ode,   - - 21

Sur les Panaches, a French Song, : - 22

A Tranflation thereof,   - - - - 24

Anfwer to the foregoing French Song,   25

Prologue fpoken at the Anchor,   - - 27

Elegy on the Death of Mr. George Smith,   28

Three Letters, on moral Subjects,   - - 31

Four Speeches deliver'd at a Literary Society, 49

A Paftoral on the Death of the Author,   59

An Elegy on the fame,   : - - 61

P O E M S

On various Subjects, &c.

E L E G Y

On the much - lamented Death of Mr.
GEORGE BLAGDEN, Attorney at Law,
Chicheſter, Febr. 14, 1773. Ætat. 23.

Stat ſua cuique dies, breve et irreparabile tempus
Omnibus eſt vitæ, ſed Famam extendere factis,
Hoc Virtutis opus.——
Virg. Æn.

IF Worth ſuperior merits our Regard,
   If Beauty faded claims the pitying Tear,
Deign then, O Muſe! to aid thy feeble Bard,
   To chant a ſolemn Dirge at BLAGDEN's Bier.

B

Attend

Attend ye Youths, whom Health and Vigour
    fire,
  Who tranfient Pleafures view with longing
    Eyes;
In this bright Copy, Virtue's Charms admire,
  And learn that Maxim, what is truly wife?

Nurs'd from the Stock with ftaid parental Care,
  The tender Cyon firm and ftately grew,
In Bloom of Life it flourifh'd heav'nly fair,
  Excell'd by none, and equall'd fcarce by few.

Warm with refin'd Good-nature was his Soul,
  His Mind adorn'd with Knowledge free from
    Pride;
With filial Piety he crown'd the whole,
  To ev'ry Grace divine by Choice ally'd.

What Hopes did from his rifing Genius flow,
  What Expectations great his Merits gave;
All, all are blafted by the fatal Blow,
  And with him bury'd in the filent Grave!

But ceafe, my Mufe, and dare no more complain,
  In fruitlefs Sighs no longer vent thy Grief;
A Lofs moft heavy, though we all fuftain,
  Religion gives an ample, fure Relief.

Heav'n's juft Decrees her facred Lips reveal;
  This Truth proclaim, our Sorrows to allay,
The due Reward of Virtue will not fail
  To crown its Vot'ries at th' appointed Day.

PSALM

PSALM I. imitated.

1.

BLEST is the Man whofe cautious Steps
   The Paths of Sin forfake;
Nor join with thofe whofe impious Lips
   A Scoff at Virtue make.

2.

But his fole Pleafure and Employ
   Is in his Maker's Law;
On that contemplates Day and Night
   With true religious Awe.

3.

As cherifh'd by refrefhing Streams,
   Which from the River glide,
The Tree with Fruit and Herbage blooms,
   In Summer's verdant Pride.

4.

So fhall the upright Man with Peace
   And profp'rous Days be crown'd;
Shall flourifh and benignly fhed
   His wholefome Fruit around.

5.

Not fo the Wicked, they from Life
   Shall rapidly be torn,

As

As Chaff by fleeting Hurricane
    From off the Earth is born.

6.

Can such before an holy Judge
    With Confidence appear?
No, struck by conscious Guilt they droop,
    Abash'd with Shame and Fear.

7.

Nor shall the Sinner with the Just
    In blissful Regions join;
Or ope his filthy Lips in Praise
    Of Majesty divine.

8.

For all the Ways of righteous Men
    The Lord with Favour views;
But those who follow wicked Steps
    His dreadful Wrath pursues.

EPITAPH

E P I T A P H

On a Brother and Sister.

STAY Mortal, stay! with deep Reflection
    read!
Nor pass, untaught, the Mansions of the Dead.
A Youth, who great in Hope, Death's Terrors
    brav'd;
A Maid, whose Innocence his Pity crav'd;
Here sleep in Dust! O! then be wise To-day;
To-morrow's Dawn may summon Thee away.

ENCOMIASTIC VERSES

On the Boarding-School for YOUNG LADIES in *Chichester.*

PIERIAN Sisters! to your Vot'ry bring
    Celestial Notes, a darling Theme to sing:
Bright Beauty, deck'd in all her native Charms,
That ev'n Detraction of her Sting disarms;
Sweet Innocence, with heav'nly Wisdom join'd,
By Education's wholesome Laws refin'd:
The highest Praise obsequious Bards pursue,
To RUSSELL's Pupils worthily is due;

                Each

While with a graceful Emulation fir'd,
Each by true Merit feeks to be admir'd,
Unus'd to ftern Compulfion's irkfome Chain,
By Diligence fair Knowledge they attain.
With Heart-felt Joy their fage Directrefs fees
A pleas'd Submiffion wait her wife Decrees;
Whofe Kindnefs, equal to maternal Love,
The grateful Smiles of Numbers well approve.
Nor lefs a Teacher's foft engaging Skill,
On tender Minds, bright Science to diftil.

Thrice happy Seminary ! where appears
A hopeful Profpect of fucceeding Years :
When Pride and Ignorance at once expell'd
Fair Beauty's Court, fhall in juft Scorn be held,
Virtue fhall fhine in elegant Array,
And all confefs her univerfal Sway.

TRUE EXCELLENCE,

AN ODE.

Virginis Os Habitumque gerens.   Virg.

LET raptur'd Bards, with Notes fublime,
     In Praife of BEAUTY tune their Lyres;
Be mine the Choice in humble Rhyme,
     To fing bright VIRTUE's nobler Fires.

Though

Though all the Cyprian Queen adore,
  Superior Charms my Sylvia grace :
Sage Wisdom's Paths her Feet explore,
  While Modesty adorns her Face.

Let Belles in Pageantry delight,
  And tinsel'd Fops their Taste approve;
In plain Attire Perfection bright
  Shall more majestically move.

Prudence most eminently shines
  In all my Charmer acts or says ;
Whilst empty Show the Maid declines,
  Her Study ever is to please.

Her Tongue base Scandal ne'er defiles ;
  What Fair, alas ! can boast the same ?
Her Soul at Calumny recoils ;
  So tender of her Neighbour's Fame.

Amid the toilsome Cares of Life,
  Content and Patience rule her Breast;
While Grandeur seeks ambitious Strife,
  Her humble Cot with Peace is blest.

What genuine Worth her Lips display !
  With what Good-nature flows her Soul !
Her Converse charms dire Spleen away,
  And dares ev'n Anger's Rage controul.

                            Maternal

Maternal Care with Joy to crown,
 How circumfpect are all her Ways !
What Tafk more worthy of Renown ?
 What more deferves fair Clio's Praife ?

O ! had I lofty Ida rang'd,
 In Place of Priam's faithlefs Son,
The haplefs Scene had then been chang'd,
 For Pallas fure the Fruit had won.

Then had old Troy fecurely ftood,
 Fair Helen ne'er with Guilt been ftain'd;
Oenone not in vain had fu'd,
 Whilft I had heav'nly Wifdom gain'd.

In Strains then equal to the Theme,
 The Woods fhould echo Sylvia's Praife,
For her alone I'd Life efteem,
 In her calm Bower clofe my Days.

FRIENDSHIP.

FRIENDSHIP.

Cui poteſt eſſe Vita vital's, qui non in Amici
mutua Benevo entia conquieſcat ?   ENNIUS.

HAIL noble FRIENDSHIP! Virtue's Off-
    ſpring hail!
Whoſe heav'nly Influence breathes into my Soul
Enthuſiaſtic Ardor! makes me dare
With tow'ring Flight PARNASSUS' Brow at-
    tempt,
Vainly preſuming all the ſacred Nine
Will join their Efforts to inſpire my Lays.

  Hail Source of Harmony and ſocial Good!
Without whoſe Stay the mightieſt Empires fall,
O'erwhelm'd with Anarchy and civil Broils!
Bereft of thee, Man ſeeks, alas! in vain,
For ſublunary Bliſs! his fondeſt Hopes
Like fumid Vapours quickly loſt in Air.

  So great thy Worth! yet how ſhall I explore
Thy ſecret Haunts, or trace thy myſtic Paths?
Far from the Verge of Courts, where Flatt'ry
    reigns,
With Speech mellifluent, Heart with Rancour
    foul;
Where ev'n the Monarch durſt not own a Friend,
Without expoſing him to public Hate;

       C   Thou

Thou tak'ft thy Flight, to feek the humble
    Bow'r,
Where dwell fair Induftry and calm Content,
Thy lovely Sifters; whence brifk COLIN hies,
With rapid Motion earneftly to feek
His Neighbour's Lambkin from the Flock far
    ftray'd;
If found, with Joy exulting home he bears
The captive Prize; with grateful Thanks repaid.
But fhould perchance the ruthlefs Spoiler feize
The helplefs Vagrant, and pollute the Plain
With crimfon Dye (irrevocable Lofs!)
With heaving Breaft and fympathizing Tears,
He mourns the dire Mifhap as if his own.

   Here in a homely, peaceable Retreat,
From bufy Scenes, in Life's autumnal Stage,
The good HONORIUS and HONESTUS dwell,
Sharing each other's Joy, each other's Grief;
Ambitious each which moft fhall pleafe his
    Friend;
Not clofer Amity refplendent once,
In fam'd ORESTES and PYLADES fhone;
Their Hopes and Fears united; nor disjoin'd
Their mutual Care to raife the drooping Soul,
By Penury depreft : grateful to him,
On whom their Life, their Happinefs depend.

                        Relax'd

Relax'd from Buf'nefs, freed from anxious
    Care,
To this fequefter'd Shade each vernal Eve,
With youthful CORYDON * my Bofom Friend,
To join in focial Converfe I retire.
Entranc'd with pleafing Wonder here we view
The beauteous Face of Nature; here admire
With facred Awe, th' unfathomable Depths
Of Providence myfterious ! Bleft Employ !
To fill the Soul with Gratitude and Love;
And fit her for refin'd celeftial Blifs.
Sometimes in artlefs rural Strains we court
The Sifter Mufes to our lov'd Retreat;
Or born on Recollection's Wing, explore
Hiftoric Annals, lafting Monuments
To worthy Characters and glorious Deeds !
Rehearfe how Heroes conquer'd, Kingdoms rofe;
What Age and Clime produc'd each great Event,
When Arts appear'd, or learned Sages wrote.
Deducing from each Subject fuch Remarks
As elevate the Mind and mend the Heart.

    Thefe thy Effects, O FRIENDSHIP, Heav'n-
    born Maid !
From thee gleam forth thofe Rays of Love
    fublime,
That dignify our Nature, crown our Hopes
With prefent Peace and future endlefs Joy :
                    Whilft

* Mr. F.

Whilſt Enmity, that hideous Monſter, Bane
Of Happineſs, that Child of loweſt Hell!
Diſgorges from her fell, rapacious Throat
Confuſion dreadful! counteracts the Laws
Of Wiſdom infinite.! and from her Womb
Emits the Children of Revenge, a Brood
Terrific! of infernal Fiends that haunt
The Soul with Guilt appall'd, embitter Life,
And add new Horror to the Pangs of Death.

   Thou Pow'r ſupreme, whoſe Influence be-
     nign
O'er all Creation's infinite Extent,
Shines forth ineffable! inſpire my Heart
With Kindneſs univerſal: let not Pride,
Envy malignant, ſordid Luſt of Gain,
Or any kindred diſcord-brooding Vice,
Diſturb my tranquil Breaſt; but let me paſs
Through all the varied Scenes which Life un-
     folds,
In ſocial Harmony with all around,
Serene and calm as glides the lucid Stream.

Congratulatory

Congratulatory Verſes,

Addreſs'd to Mr. WILLIAM FARLEY, _Chicheſter_, on his happy Recovery from the Small Pox.

Ex illo Corydon, Corydon eſt Tempore nobis.

VIRG. Ecl.

SINCE CORYDON from dire Contagion freed,
  Again with blooming Vigour tunes his
    Reed
To dulcet Strains, ſhall I, his Friend, refuſe
The early Gratulations of my Muſe?
Rather, lov'd Genius, be th' Occaſion bleſt,
On which my warm Eſteem ſhall be expreſt,
Ere yet the modeſt Veil of Youth withdrawn,
Diſplays thy Merit as the ſmiling Dawn;
Ere the fair Flow'r is in Perfection blown,
Or to the World it's op'ning Splendor known.
But ceaſe dull Praiſe, too weak thy Fame to
    ſpread,
Accept my earneſt Wiſhes in its Stead.
Smooth glide thy Days, with all thoſe Joys
    replete,
Which conſcious Virtue ever will await:
Long in the Sphere of Science may'ſt thou move,
The Height of Nature's Excellence to prove;

In

In Doubts to lead the Ignorant aright.
And place true Wifdom in its proper Light :
Here to reform at once and charm Mankind,
(A Tafk well fuited to thy noble Mind),
And fhed refplendent Luftre on an Age,
In which Vice triumphs with unbounded Rage.
O! may the Deftinies thy Thread extend,
And gracious Heav'n each needful Bleffing
    lend,
To crown with Peace thy Life, Felicity thy
    End.

T O

The Rev. Mr. W-lk-r,

On hearing him Preach at Chichefter Cathedral, April 30th, 177.

Quicquid dignum fapiente bonoque eft. Hor.

A Youthful Bard, as yet to thee unknown,
(Whofe Mufe on meritorious Themes alone
Empl.ys her Art) attempts, in humble Verfe,
Thy Worth and Skill tranfcendent to rehearfe.

No more the Bar, the Senate, and the Stage,
To their fole Aid fhall Eloquence engage;
               In

In THEE her Charms the sacred Roftrum grace,
Where far more noble Subjects claim a Place:
There Arguments, with pow'rful Motives fraught,
Enforce the Truths thy heav'nly Mafter taught,
With all the Strength of Elocution join'd,
To fix Attention in the wand'ring Mind.

While Zeal enthufiaftic vents aloud,
With frantic Gefture, to the trembling Croud,
Tenets abfurd, *thy* pious Accents fire
Our languid Souls, excite us to admire
Religion's Afpect, pleafant and benign,
And own its holy Maxims all divine.
Nor with lefs Energy thy Lips relate
Th' impending Horrors of a finful State;
Teach us the direful Rocks of Vice to fhun,
On which fo many fatally have run.

Thrice happy they whom thy wife Counfels
      lead,
Where Virtue dwells, in heav'nly Charms array'd;
Who quit the Paths of Mifery and Shame
To feek immortal Blifs, and endlefs Fame.

Still, Rev'rend Youth, continue to impart
The pure, the wholefome Dictates of thy Heart.
Religion to its priftine Splendor raife,
And by thy great Example fmooth its Ways;
Thus may'ft thou here thy holy Function grace,
And, after Death, eternal Joys embrace.

An Hymn of Gratitude.

TO thee my Saviour, God, and King,
.I confecrate my humble Lays,
With feeble Voice I fain would fing
  My Great, Sublime Creator's Praife.

But how fhall I the Lord Supreme
  , In Language fuitable addrefs ?
What Words will reach the lofty Theme,
  Immortal Majefty exprefs !

Affift me Heav'n, and tune my Lyre
  With Notes angelic from above;
Do thou my glowing Breaft infpire
  With Raptures of extatic Love.

From Thee all Excellence I trace;
  To Thee all Nature's Glory tends,
Sweet Fountain of celeftial Grace,
  On whom alone true Blifs depends.

At thy omnipotent Decree
  The Univerfe from nothing rofe,
And all its beauteous Parts agree
  Their glorious Author to difclofe.

And fhall not I, in grateful Strains,
  Thy Wifdom, Goodnefs, Pow'r difplay ?
Whofe Providence my Life fuftains,
  Enrich'd with Mercies Day by Day.

From

From Infancy to Age mature,
　My Guide and Comfort haft thou prov'd;
Guarded by thee I reft fecure,
　Each Fear and Danger far remov'd.

When dire Difeafe my languid Frame
　With Pain and Mifery oppreft,
To my Relief thy Pity came,
　And balmy Health my Vitals bleft.

Unvex'd with every anxious Care,
　That Wealth or Indigence await,
Amply thy bounteous Gifts I fhare,
　With fweet Tranquility replete.

But O! thy vaft tranfcendent Love,
　To me and all Mankind difplay'd,
When from the glorious Realms above,
　In meek Humility array'd,

The Great Meffias came, to clear
　The Mift which long fair Truth obfcur'd,
Our Souls with blifsful Hopes to chear,
　In Guilt and Mifery immur'd.

O bleft Redemption! hallow'd Sound!
　The balmy Comfort of my Soul;
In thee unfading Joys abound;
　Pleafures on endlefs Pleafures roll.

To feek O Lord! thy wonted Grace,
　Let Gratitude my Heart excite;

D　　　　　　　　　Difplay

Display the Glories of thy Face,
   And guide my wand'ring Steps aright.

That I the blest seraphic Choir,
   In Concert may hereafter join,
And tune the ever-sacred Lyre,
   In grateful Praise of Love divine.

AD AMICUM †.

NUNC age, excussis Animo, Sodalis,
   Tristibus Curis, virides relinque
BELGICÆ * Gentis variis nitentes
           Messibus Agros.

Hic bibes mecum recubans Falernum,
Et fruens ulmi placidâ Quiete
Arva quà lambit saliente Lymphâ
           Vitreus Amnis.

Igneos Ictus viridans repellet
Otiosis Sylva, et amœna leni
Aura spirabit Zephyri Susurro
           Pectori Amorem.

† This Poem is taken from SYLVÆ, or a Collection
of POEMS, by a Young Gentleman of Chichester.

* Veteres Hantoniæ incolæ appellabantur Belgæ

Panque

Panque montanus, celeresque Fauni,
Ac decens Nympharum aderunt Caterva,
Dum canis Flacci Citharâ faceti
                              Digna Mariæ.

Occupemus sic fugitiva Vitæ
Gaudia. --- An nobis, quid Iberus ardens,
Quidve Galli frustrà agitent Minaces
                              Mente dolosâ ?

Torva quas Umbras cruciet MEGÆRA?
Quas strepens Oras feriatve TETHYS ?
Quas Deûm Rex nunc jaculetur Arces
                              Fulmine misso ?

Dum licit, labens patiturque Tempus,
Flore præcincti Caput, accinamus
Fervidos Ignes, minimè anxii quid
                              Cura futura.

Translation by D. F. Junr.

TO MY FRIEND.

COME now my Friend, while Youth re-
        mains,
   Let anxious Cares desert thy Breast ;
Forsake awhile HANTONIA's Plains, .
   In Summer's various Beauties drest.

Beneath

Beneath a verdant Shade reclin'd,
  With me the grateful Time employ,
Where limpid Rills their Courses wind,
  Falernian Juice shall raise our Joy.

Now shelter'd from the scorching Ray,
  We'll taste the Pleasures of the Grove,
Where Zephyrus in wanton Play,
  Shall breathe the genuine Sweets of Love :

While Mountain PAN and sprightly Fauns
  Attend thy soft *Horatian* Lyre,
With Nymphs that grace the flow'ry Lawns,
  MARIA shall the Song inspire.

Thus let us grasp the fleeting Hours,
  That yet with purest Transports teem,
Nor dread what Mischiefs foreign Pow'rs
  'Gainst *Albion*'s Safety vainly scheme.

Within our calm Retreat secure,
  No fears shall discompose the Mind ;---
What Ghosts infernal Pangs endure,
  To stern MEGÆRA's Chains consign'd,

Concern us not,--- nor 'gainst what Shore
  The rushing Waves impetuous move,
O'er what doom'd Fortress Thunders roar,
  Hurl'd by the Arm of angry Jove.

Whilst Time and Freedom are our own,
  Let us our Loves in Songs declare,
With flow'ry Wreaths our Temples crown,
  Regardless of To-morrows Care.   T H E

THE FIRST OF MAY,

AN ODE.

THE fmiling Seafon now appears,
   All Nature greets the welcome Day,
That each defponding Mortal chears,
   The lovely, grateful Firft of May.

The Trees, adorn'd with varied Bloom,
   The chearful Warblers on the Spray,
The Flow'rs, exhaling rich Perfume,
   All hail the welcome Firft of May.

The wanton Herds now tofs their Heads,
   And fprightly Lambkins frifk and play,
Light-bounding o'er th' enamell'd Meads,
   Charm'd with the grateful Firft of May.

Stern Boreas now no longer reigns,
   Bright PHOEBUS rules with lenient Sway,
And gilds the Mountains, Woods and Plains,
   To crown the joyful Firft of May.

Soft Zephyrs too, in gentle Gales,
   Chafe wintry Vapours far away,
And breathing Fragrance o'er the Vales,
   Embalm the lovely Firft of May.

See

See how the jovial Swains advance,
  With Nymphs, adorn'd in Liv'ries gay,
To join the annual blithfome Dance,
  And celebrate the Firft of May.

Around where ftands the ftately Pole,
  With Garlands deck'd in bright Array,
Pleafure and Mirth infpire the whole,
  To greet with Songs the Firft of May.

Hafte then, dear Sylvia, to thy Swain,
  Through flow'ry Meadows let us ftray,
Exchange our mutual Vows again,
  And crown with Love the Firft of May.

SUR LES PANACHES,

CHANSON.

Addreffee aux Dames de CHICHESTER,

(AIR, *Revelles vous belle Endormie.*)

OUI fur la Tête de vos Dames
    Laiffes les Panaches floter ;
Ils font analogues aux Femmes,
  Elles font bien de les porter.

La

La Femme se peint elle même
   Dans ce frivol Ajuftement ;
La Plume vole elle eft l'Emblême
   De ce Sexe trop inconftant.

Des Femmes l'on fçait les Coutumes ;
   Vous font elles quelque Serment ?
Fiés vous y comme a leurs Plumes
   Autant en emporte le Vent.

D'un Panache moins ridicule
   Le Mulet marche revêtu,
Qui de la Femme ou de la Mule
   Eft l'Animal le plus têtu ?

La Femme auffi du haut Parage
   Porte Plumes chès les Incas,
Mais chès eux la Femme eft fauvage,
   Et les votres ne le font pas.

Si vous ornés en Engleterre
   D'un Panache votre Moitié
D'un autre, d'un autre Matiere
   On la voit vous gratifié.

The

The Plume of Feathers,

A SONG.

Addrefs'd to the Ladies of CHICHESTER.

(Tranflated by D. F. Junr.)

THAT Feathers well become the Fair
    No Cenfor can di.pute,
They, ruffled by each Breath of Air,
    Such wav'ring Tempers fuit.

No jufter Emblem of the Mind
    Can outward Shew impart,
Than, pictur'd in her Drefs we find
    A faithlefs Woman's Heart.

When fhe her ufual Vows prefumes
    With Fondnefs to declare,
Believe them ftable as her Plumes
    That float about in Air.

The Mule, with grateful Plumage crown'd
    In ftately Pomp is led;
Say, which is by Experience found
    To wear the ftrongeft Head?

What

What though the rich Peruvian Dame
   Her Crown with Feathers grace,
Muft Britifh Ladies act the fame
   As this vile favag Race.

Then Englifhmen, this Counfel take,
   Such paltry Toys defpife,
Left on your Brow they foon fhould make,
   Some other Plumage rife.

Anfwer to the foregoing French Song.

By *D. FOOT*, Junr.

WHAT, fhall a foreign Critic dare
    With Freedom to reprove
The Manners of the Britifh Fair,
   And not our Cenfure move ?

Forbid it Beauty, and each Grace
   That dignifies the Sex,
Nor let the Stings of Satire bafe
   Celeftial Minds perplex.

Shall Britain's Daughters to the Mules
   Of Gallia be compar'd ?
Farewell, then, Modefty ! thy Rules
   Are obfelete declar'd.

E   Prefumptuous

Prefumptuous Bard! fay, whence arife
   Thy Hatred and thy Spite?
Canft thou thofe Heav'nly Charms defpife
   Which give each Breaft Delight.

But why amidft the Feather'd Train,
   Diftinguifh'd from the reft,
Should fair CICESTRIA's Dames retain
   The Stigma of thy Jeft?

Is it that Affectation here
   Alone her Pomp difplays?
Or that fuperior Charms appear,
   And Envy fwells thy Lays?

THY Country more deferves the Stings
   Of fuch opprobrious Rhymes,
From whence the Drefs fantaftic fprings,
   The Vice of modern Times.

To HER then let thy Mufe return,
   Her empty Tafte revile;
Nor longer let thy Malice burn
   Againft this happy Ifle.

JULY 26th, 1776.

PROLOGUE,

PROLOGUE,

Spoken by the Author at the Annual Feaſt
of a MUSICAL SOCIETY held at the
Anchor Inn, in *Chicheſter, February*
the 28th, 1775.

TO-Day the annual feſtive Board is crown'd;
   Let genial Mirth and Friendſhip ſmile a-
   around.
To-day the Sons of Harmony unite
Their vocal Strains, diffuſive of Delight.
CICESTRIA's Choir the wide Expance ſhall rend,
Whilſt liſt'ning Warblers on the Spray attend.
With ſweet melodius Pipe ſhall BARBER charm,
And ORPHEUS-like, e'en ſavage Force diſarm.
In deep ſonorous Note ſhall CARTER join,
And deck with Majeſty the flowing Line.
Diſpell'd be Grief, briſk Mirth diffus'd around,
When tuneful PASCO, BARNARD, BUTTON ſound,
In lively Catch, or ſmiling ſocial Glee :
Say, Critics, where their Equals ſhall we ſee ?
When LUFFE's enchanting Accents fill the Skies,
Each Senſe is loſt in Rapture and Surpriſe.
Nor ſhall the tender Lays of MECKETT loſe
Their juſt Regard, the Tribute of the Muſe;

E 2   In

In native Melody fupreme he fhines,
Whilft Innocence adorns his rural Lines.

Hail matchlefs Band! in fweet Accord con-
    fpire,
Each Heart with glowing Extacy to fire.
Let Wit and Love their grateful Numbers join,
And add frefh Luftre to the fparkling Wine.
Difcord avaunt! fly far ye Cares away!
Let tuneful PHOEBUS, ever young and gay,
His Beams benignly fhed, to crown the blith-
    fome Day.

E L E G Y

On the Death of Mr. GEORGE SMITH,
Landfcape Painter, of *Chichefter*, *Sep-*
tember 7th, 1776.

———— Præcipe lugubres,
Cantus, Melpomene.—— HOR. Carm. 24. Lib. I.

Multum ille quidem flebilis occidit.   Ibid.

CEleftial Nine! your mournful Strains unite,
   With folemn Mufic tune your facred Lyres;
And aid my feeble Numbers to recite
  How great a Lofs each plaintive Breaft in-
    fpires.

The Lofs of SMITH ! whofe Merits well demand,
  The utmoft Skill of Eloquence and Verfe,
To fhield his Mem'ry from Oblivion's Hand,
  And to fucceeding Times his Praife rehearfe,

Yet why ?--- his Works alone fhall fpread his
    Fame,
  And tell his Worth to ev'ry diftant Age;
Nor need fuch feeble Efforts to proclaim
  The Truths that crown his own immortal
    Page,

In him the Sifter Arts united fhone :---
  His Pencil ev'n might TITIAN's Skill out-
    vie :---
His Tints, excell'd by Nature's Self alone,
  At once aftonifh and delight the Eye.

Thrice only, Candidate for publick Fame,
  His matchlefs Skill the Laurels THRICE * at-
    tain'd,
His Works the Glory of the Age became,
  And endlefs Honour for their Mafter gain'd.

In native Eafe and Innocence array'd,
  His rural Notes enraptur'd ev'ry Ear,
And well the Goodnefs of his Heart portray'd,
  The MAN, the Chriftian, and the Friend fin-
    cere.

---

* Alludes to his getting the Premium three times.

Nor

Nor lefs the Charms of Mufic (heav'nly Art !)
   His Skill difplay'd in foft, harmonious Strains,
Strains that might ev'n diffolve the favage Heart,
   And bind the captive Soul in pleafing Chains.

Weep on, fair Science, for thy favour'd Son,
   The laft Survivor of the illuftrious Three†;
Too foon, alas! the glorious Prize he won,
   And left difconfolate his Friends and thee.

Let Britain too her heavy Lofs deplore,
   A Genius, whofe unrivall'd Works impart
Her num'rous Graces to each diftant Shore,
   And ftile her Queen of ev'ry noble Art.

And thou, bright Virtue! lend thy heav'nly
     Aid;
   With choiceft Gifts adorn his facred Shrine,
Who ne'er from thy delightful Borders ftray'd,
   But trod the unerring Paths of Truth divine.

† Three Brothers, all Capital Painters.

THREE

THREE LETTERS.

. LETTER I.

DEAR BROTHER,

A S it concerns us all (and more especially near Relations) to promote as much as possible the Welfare of each other, accept these my poor Endeavours for that Purpose; which I beg You will read and confider with Attention. My Defign is to lay before You fome Rules, which being duly regarded, will fecure us a prefent and everlafting Felicity; and which (I am forry to fay,) many of us, though not unacqainted with, treat with too much Negligence. Though I fhall come far Short of that Excellency which fo interefting a Subject requires, yet I flatter myfelf the good Intention will be an Excufe for the Faults, and will (by Divine Bleffing) produce the wifh'd-for Effect.

Our All-wife Creator hath implanted in us a Divine Faculty called Reafon, to guide us in the Purfuit of thofe Things which are moft for our real Advantage; and hath alfo favour'd us with his revealed Will in the facred Scriptures, to direct us farther than the Extent of Human Reafon;

fon: There the meaneft of us may difcover
with Eafe, what the greateft Philofophers of Old
had but the fainteft Glimmerings of. To make
a right Ufe of thefe ineftimable Bleffings is the
beft Return we can make, and all that he requires of us; on this depends our eternal Happinefs or Mifery. Now can there be any thing
more agreeable to the Dictates of Reafon, than
that we fhould offer the utmoft Adoration to
that Omnipotent, Omnifcient, All-gracious Being, who underftands all our Thoughts, Words
and Actions; who is always nigh to them that
call upon him faithfully; to thank him for the
many Bleffings we continually receive from his
bounteous Hand; to implore Pardon for the
unworthy Returns we often make to his infinite
Love and Mercy; to beg his Bleffing on our ho-
neft Defigns and Undertakings, and his gracious Affiftance in working out our Salvation?
But this is enforc'd by our Saviour in the Gof-
pel with the moft preffing and promifing Terms;
" Afk and it fhall given You; feek and ye fhall
find." "Whatfoever Ye fhall afk the Father in
my Name, he will give it You." 'Tis this eafy
profitable Duty that is the Foundation of true
Piety; 'Tis this that peculiarly diftinguifhes
Men from Brutes; and will be a means of ob-
taining the Divine Favour to lead us in the
Paths of Happinefs. And we ought to have
efpecial

efpecial Regard to it every Night and Morning;
for innumerable Dangers are continually over
our Heads, and we are not fure that each Day
may not be our laft; but if by Prayer, when
we go to reft, we have made an Atonement to
God for our Sins; committed ourfelves to his
Fatherly Protection, with a firm Refolution to
amend our Lives, we are fecure againft the
worft that may happen; no Terrors can affright
us, no Dangers hurt us, and even Death itfelf
cannot reach our immortal Part. And when
we arife, our unfeigned Thanks are due to him
for preferving us the Night paft, and raifing us
up in Health and Safety, befeeching him to
protect us thro' the Day from all Sin and Danger. No Excufe fhould ever hinder us from
the Difcharge of this Duty, in publick and private; for as nothing is of fo great Advantage as
God's Favour, nothing is fo terrible as his Dif-
pleafure. If we feek him, he will be found of
us, but if we forfake him he will caft us off for
ever.

But as in our Devotions we are to ufe the
facred Name of God with the greateft Reverence, fo we are ftrictly forbid to prophane it.
" The Lord will not hold him guiltlefs that ta-
keth his Name in vain." This is the Almighty's pofitive Decree, and cannot be rever'd.
How much then is it to be lamented that many
have fo accuftom'd themfelves to this wicked

F   Habit,

Habit, that they can scarcely utter a Word without an Oath; and in their common Discourse are for ever blaspheming God. 'Tis not only the greatest Impiety but the highest Pitch of Folly, for could one of these Persons see his ordinary Discourse in Writing, it must make the most Ignorant ashamed. Let me then advise You never to be guilty of this great Wickedness. Bad Customs are easily acquired, but very difficult to shake off. If every idle Word that Men shall speak will be accounted for at the Day of Judgement, with what Horror shall such Persons appear before that tremendous Judge, whose Name they have so often derided.

Next to God, the utmost Reverence is due to our Parents. No Duty can be more reasonable than this. 'Tis to them under God we are indebted for our Being, and Preservation from our Birth; many Toils and Afflictions have they suffer'd for our Sakes; many laborious Days and restless Nights. In our Infancy and Sickness they have nurs'd us with the greatest Tenderness and Care; our Welfare have been their Joy, our Misfortunes their Grief: for which (tho' we cannot make them sufficient Return) let us endeavour to shew the sincerest Gratitude, in assisting them to our utmost; performing their Commands with Pleasure, not despising

their

their Reproofs, but submitting to their better
Judgement. So shall we one Day receive the
due Reward of this our filial Piety, and may
possibly hereafter also be blest with Children as
good as we ourselves have been.

We are also commanded to love our Neigh-
bours as ourselves; to do to all Men as we
would have them do to us; not to envy but honour our Superiors, and be friendly and kind to
our Inferiors and Equals. Not to be malicious
when injur'd, but to forgive our Enemies, and
do them all the good Offices in our Power.
Our Obedience to these Precepts will prove us
to be true Disciples of our Saviour, by following
his blessed Steps, who prayed for his Enemies
under the most cruel Torments; " Father, forgive them for they know not what they do."

I have now given a short Sketch of our princi-
pal Duties to God and our Neighbour, which
you may see more clearly laid out and inforced
in several pious Books; but in the New Testa-
ment we may find not only the best and most
important Precepts, but also such a blessed Example of the Practice of them, as is beyond the
Power of Man to give. There we may see the Son
of God himself, who knew no Sin, condescend
to take upon him our Nature, suffer the greatest Hardships and Miseries of Life, and the most

cruel and ignominious Death, as a Sacrifice for
our Sins; leaving us the brighteft Pattern of
Holinefs to copy after, and a fure Means of Re-
conciliation with God, Repentance thro' his
Name, who is now at the Right Hand of God,
always interceding for penitent Offenders. Let
us therefore turn unto him, and feek him while
he may be found, that fo we may obtain his
Grace to help us in Time of Need. Let us attend his Worfhip with Reverence and Humility;
Hear his holy Word attentively, and obey it
with Sincerity and Love. 'Tis not (as fome
foolifhly imagine) a hard Tafk to ferve God;
he is not a fevere and rigid Tafk-Mafter, exaĉt-
ing more from us than we can perform: No,
the Ways of Religion are Ways of Pleafantnefs,
and all its Paths are Peace; his Yoke is eafy,
and his Burden is light. And could we once
be perfuaded to make the Trial, we fhould foon
be convinced that he who lives in the conftant
Fear and Love of his Maker, fhews his utmoft
Endeavour to obey his Commands, is in Friendfhip and Charity with all Mankind, is diligent in his Calling, contented in his Situation,
true and juft in all his Aĉtions; tho' his outward Circumftances are but mean and defpica-
ble, has yet more fubftantial and real Happinefs
than Riches or the greateft worldly Gratificati-
ons can beftow. No Affliĉtions can difturb the
Peace

Peace of a good Confcience; it will advance us above the Reach of the greateft Troubles, and make our Souls happy when our Bodies are in Mifery : whereas fhould a wicked Man have the greateft Profperity in the World, he is yet unhappy ; his Confcience difturbs and haunts him wherever he goes ; he feels not the leaft Satisfaction in Riches, but is in want of that which Wealth cannot buy ; his Life is continually uneafy, and Death, inftead of relieving, will lead him to much greater and more lafting Torments. While to a good Man it proves only the exchanging of a vain and troublefome World, for the delightful Regions of eternal Happinefs. A proper Confideration on this, one might think, would reclaim the moft harden'd Sinner, and make him chufe the pleafant Paths of Virtue. Let me advife you therefore to Remember your Creator in the Days of your Youth; to apply your Heart to true Wifdom, which is the Fear of the Lord ; to check your unruly Paffions, and unlawful Defires ; quit the broad Way which leads to Mifery, and walk in the ftrait Way which leads to Life eternal.

But whilft I am admonifhing you, I hope I fhall not be found one of thofe who give Rules to others which themfelves will not practice, and are ready to pull the Mote out of their Brother's

Eye,

Eye, but perceive not the Beam in their own. No, I am truly fenfible of the many grievous Offences I have been guilty of, for which I am heartily forry and afhamed; but I hope by fincere Repentance, and a future virtuous Life, thro' the Interceffion of our Redeemer, we fhall both be received to Divine Favour, and be in the Number of thofe, who fhall be pronounced Bleffed at the Great Day of Retribution. I am

Your loving Brother,

Sincere Friend and Well-wifher,

CHICHESTER,
April 2d, 1771.

D. FOOT,

LETTER II.

Dear BROTHER,

ONCE more I offer you my poor, though well intended Advice; and intreat you as a Brother and a Friend, if you have any Regard for your real Intereft, to confider ferioufly what I now lay before you. Should any one direct you how to acquire an immenfe Fortune, would you not gratefully follow fuch Advice? how
much

much more when the Means are given you to obtain thofe Riches which fhall never fail, thofe Pleafures which fhall never have an End. The Tafk is not difficult; our Gracious Creator hath put it into every one's Power to be for ever happy, and it is our own Fault if we will not embrace the Opportunity while we have it. Remember how fhort and uncertain our Time is! how foon we may be called to give a folemn Account of our Actions before the Searcher of all Hearts! Though we are now in the Bloom of Youth and Health, yet many are the Accidents by which we, as well as others, may be cut off; perhaps To-day or To-morrow may be our laft; a few Years at moft will put a Period to our Exiftence; and whether we are prepared or not, will bring us to that great Tribunal, where all our Thoughts, Words and Actions will be examin'd, and eternal Happinefs or Mifery await the irrevocable Sentence we fhall then receive.

In my laft I gave you a fhort Summary of our neceffary Chriftian Duties, with fome few Remarks on the Advantages arifing from the Obfervance of them. I fhall now enlarge a little further on the Duty we owe to God as our Creator, Preferver, Governor, and kind Benefactor; hoping this will make a proper Impref-
fion

fion on your Mind, and by the Divine Blefling
lead you back from the Paths of Sin and Mifery, into the Ways of Virtue, of Pleafantnefs,
and of Peace.

To know and believe in God is the Foundation of all Religion ; that is, to obtain, by fre-
quent Meditations on his Divine Nature and
Perfections, fuch a Knowledge of and Faith in
Him, as may produce in us a fincere Defire to
obey his Will. If we reflect on his infinite
Power, that he created all things out of nothing by the Word of his Mouth ; that he can
as eafily put a Period to their Exiftence ; that
he cafteth down the Mighty and exalteth the
lowly ; that he can cut us off in the Midft of
our Sins, and plunge us into everlafting Deftruction ; certainly thefe Confiderations muft
fufficiently humble us, remind us of own Im-
potency, and make us cautious not to offend
him. His infinite Wifdom, fo confpicuous
through all his Works, in which nothing is imperfect, but every thing fhews forth its Divine
Author, muft create in us the higheft Reverence
and Refpect for Him ; teach us to be contented and thankful in that Situation which he hath
placed us, and patiently fubmiffive to his Divine Will under every Difpenfation, not doubt-
ing but if we fincerely love and ferve him, he
will make all things work together for our Good.

A.

A Contemplation on his infinite Goodnefs and Mercy, fo often difplayed to us unworthy Sinners, in conferring on us all things neceffary for our Comfort and Convenience; bleffing us with Health, Friends, Food and Raiment; giving us the noble Endowments of Reafon and Underftanding, muft awaken in us the finçereft Gratitude and Affection. But to what Rapture of Love and Admiration will our Hearts be raifed, if we confider as we ought, that amazing Inftance of his exceeding Kindnefs and Compaffion for us, our Redemption from the Bondage of Sin, by the Sacrifice of his only Son! who gave himfelf up to a cruel and ignominious Death, that he might obtain for us eternal Life. And when we are faft bound with the Chains of Iniquity, carry'd away by every Temptation, and ready to fink under our Burden, how tranfporting is the Reflection that we have a Saviour and Redeemer at hand, who, upon our Repentance and Refolution of Amendment, will intercede for us, reftore us again to Favour, and affift our weak and imperfect Endeavours. If we behold a wife, virtuous, or powerful Perfon with Admiration, Love and Refpect, let us remember what Veneration and Efteem is due to him who is the King of Kings, and is the Source from whence every good and perfect Gift is deriv'd.

G

Thefe

These Reflections, affifted by a diligent Attention to the Holy Scriptures, will introduce us to fuch a Knowledge and Senfe of the Nature and Attributes of God, and our neceffary Dependence upon him, as will lead us to the Practice of our religious and moral Duties: But obferve this Truth, (which the Experience of every Day has fully proved) that thofe who put not their Truft in God, but live in a Courfe of continual Impiety and Irreligion, are feldom (if ever) otherwife than defective in Juftice and Charity to their Brethren. Againft thefe Perfons, human Laws were made; for, the Laws of God and Confcience are fufficient to warn a Man from the Danger of fecret as well as notorious Sins, and direct him to fuch Actions as are virtuous and praife-worthy. We learn from the before mentioned Guides to worfhip our Creator in Spirit and in Truth; to adore him as well with the Heart as by the outward Geftures of Humility; to beg of him what is needful for our Souls and Bodies, and thank him for the many Mercies and Bleffings we have already received; and as we continually ftand in need of his gracious Affiftance and Protection, are every Moment favour'd with frefh Inftances of his Goodnefs, fo we never fhould be wanting in our Petitions for the Continuance of thefe Mercies; fince he who is Truth itfelf has promifed, that

if

if we afk faithfully, we fhall obtain effectually.
And when the Almighty invites and commands,
fhall we weak Mortals refufe to obey! Can
any of us be fo daring as to lie down in our
Beds without imploring his gracious Protection,
and Pardon for our Sins, when we know not
whether we fhall ever fee the Morning Light?
Do we arife in Health and Safety, refrefhed
and fit for our daily Employments, and fhall
we not with bended Knees offer up our Thankf-
givings to the Author of thefe Favors? Can
we proceed on our worldly Concerns without
begging his Affiftance and Support? Shall we
receive our daily Suftenan e without remember-
ing and acknowledging the Giver of all good
Things? And yet (fhocking is the Thought!)
how many neglect thefe weighty Matters! how
many eat and drink, lie down and rife, as if
they had no more Reafon or Reflection than the
Beafts that perifh! Depending on themfelves
and Friends, they forget their great Benefactor, difregard his Ordinances, and defpife the
Offers of his Grace. Even the Day which he
hath order'd to be kept facred to divine Purpofes, they, by Riot, Drunkennefs, and De-
bauchery, make too often the moft unholy of
all the feven; or if, perhaps, they do not always break out into fuch flagrant Enormities,
they do not confider that the Neglect of Wor-

fhip,

ſhip, of hearing and reading God's holy Word,
and ſpending the Sabbath in vain Pleaſures and
worldly Concerns, is a ſhameful Profanation of
it, and a Breach of a poſitive Commandment.
But be not deceived: theſe Matters, though
they may appear trifling in the Eyes of inconſi-
derate Men, are not ſo with God. He hath
furniſhed us with Reaſon to inſtruct us in what
is right and profitable for us; hath revealed to
us his Will in the holy Scriptures; hath made
the Ways of Virtue conducive to the moſt ſolid
Comfort and Enjoyment here, as well as to
eternal Happineſs hereafter; hath offered us his
gracious Aſſiſtance to further our weak Endeavours, and conduct us thro' the ſeveral Stages
of our Duty. If we are regardleſs of all theſe
Mercies, are deaf to his Promiſes and Threat-
nings, and reſolve to continue impenitent, what
can we expect but the fierce Vengeance of his
Wrath and heavy Diſpleaſure? Who, if they
would but ſeriouſly conſider that they have it in
their Power to enjoy an Eternity of Happineſs,
would be ſo ſtupid as to chooſe eternal Miſery?
O that Men were wiſe, and conſider'd often
their latter End! That they would frequently
meditate on a future State, and compare impar-
tially their temporal with their eternal Intereſt!
then would every one ſtrive to live as he would
wiſh to die. The ſhort Time of our Continuance

ance here would be improved in pious and bene-
volent Actions, and happy should be our Condition even in this Life: But since by the Frail-
ty of our Nature, we cannot hope to arrive at
such universal Perfection in this Scene of
Things, let us, who have no Excuse for our
Neglect, but every Advantage to forward us in
the Way of Salvation, endeavour, by a constant
Attention to those Precepts which are given us
by our Creator himself, to obtain that glorious
Prize, the Testimony of a good Conscience,
which shall bea us up under every Affliction,
comfort us in the Hour of Death, and introduce us to the blessed Society of Saints in the
glorious Regions of Bliss and Immortality.

I am,

Your loving Brother,

CHICHESTER,
August 31st, 1771.

D. FOOT.

LETTER III.

DEAR BROTHER,

I Received yours, and am greatly pleased with
your Remarks on the Exhibitions at the
Theatre and Sadler's Wells. But I find your
Curiosity

Curiofity has furnifhed me with a Subject for a few Words, by way of Admonition, which I hope you will accept as from one who fincerely wifhes your Welfare.

.... Thefe Entertainments, to one who never be fore faw London, and is willing to indulge himfelf in a moderate Way, may perhaps not be dangerous; but beware of placing your Affections on fuch Objects. Vice, tho' the moft deteftable Monfter in Nature, generally appears in the moft alluring and engaging Forms, and the moft wary are oftentimes entangled in her Snares. In an Age of Luxury and Diffipation, he who fuffers himfelf to be carried away by the Tide of Fafhion and the general Cuftoms of thofe around him, will moft certainly fuffer Shipwreck, as many of thofe unhappy Wretches you mention'd have fadly experienced. No, let the Wicked and Profligate laugh at your Virtue and Prudence (or Singularity if they pleafe to call it), you will one Day have fufficient Reafon to mourn their Folly and approve your own wife Refolutions. Whilft the Pleafures of the World (if they may be ftiled Pleafures) are attended with Uneafinefs, Anxieties, and Difappointments, continue but for a Moment, and are followed by a long Train of Evils; the Pleafures of Virtue are real, fubftanti-

al,

al, and full of folid Satisfaction, undisturbed by
the greatest Troubles, and what is more, of infinite Duration. Surely then, if there were
fewer noble Examples for our Imitation, who
would not even appear fingular in his Choice,
when the Balance is fo much in his Favour?
But if you carefully examine, you may find in
London a fufficient Number of agreeable and
improving Acquaintance. Mr. S——, your
Mafter (I am inform'd) is a worthy Gentleman: endeavour by your faithful and obliging
Behaviour to conciliate his Efteem; and you
will doubtlefs find in him not only a good Mafter, but a fincere Friend. With Mr. R——,
and his Spoufe you will fee Frugality and Good-
nature in their greateft Perfection. In the Com-
pany of Mr. D—— you will moft probably learn
Sobriety and Difcretion; Virtues which he pof-
feffed in a confpicuous Manner when at Chichefter. In the Converfation of fuch Perfons you
will find more folid Entertainment than in the
the moft pleafing Exhibitions.

In the Bufinefs of your Profeffion let not your
Views be contracted within the narrow Limits
of a Journeyman. You have been blefs'd with
a tolerable good Education; and I hope Providence will one Day put it in your Power to
move in a more enlarged Sphere: therefore it
highly concerns you to let no Opportunity flip
of

of getting a juft Notion of Trade; to make yourfelf not only Mafter of your Bufinefs, but to find out every Place where any of the Articles you ufe may be bought at the beft Hand; and make proper Minutes of them; to liften attentively when Trade is the Topick of Converfation, you may catch hold of fomething that may be of infinite Service to you. It behoves you not only to acquire a good Notion of your own Trade, but to furnifh yourfelf with the Knowledge of Trade in general: poffibly you may hit on fomething that may be much more to your Advantage than that you are at prefent engaged in, or which may be added to it by an induftrious Application.

With regard to Curiofities, look round Weftminfter Abbey, behold the Monarchs, the Heroes and Sages of our Nation, and while you read the recorded Virtues of thofe great, and extraordinary Charaéters, you muft remember, that it will be your Duty as well as Intereft, to " Go and do likewife." I am

Your loving Brother,

CHICHESTER,
September 29, 1772.   D. FOOT.

SPEECHES

Deliver'd at a LITERARY SOCIETY
in Chichefter.

GENTLEMEN,

THE Queftion intended for this Evening's
Difcuffion is, " Whether is there any fuch
" thing as Happinefs in the World? if there
" is, where is it to be found ? "

If by Happinefs is meant an entire Exempti-
on from Pain and Trouble, and a continual
Succeffion of Delights, capable neither of A-
batement nor Allay, I am confident that the u-
niverfal Voice of Mankind will fupport my O-
pinion, that there is no fuch thing in the World.
Such a State of pure and perfect Blifs can only
be expected in thofe happy Manfions where Perfection ever reigns.   The utmoft of human
Happinefs can only be eftimated by Compari-
fon, that is, one Perfon may enjoy, or feem to
enjoy, a greater Portion of it than another.
Though this has ever been the chief Purfuit of
all Mankind, few, very few are fo fortunate as
to obtain a moderate Degree of it; and the
Reafon is clearly evident, the Generality of them
follow

follow a wrong Courfe. It is no Wonder, therefore, that they are often " loft and bewilder'd
" in the fruitlefs Search." Some fancy it is to
be found in Honours and Titles; others in O-
pulence and Grandeur; many in Pleafure, Eafe,
and Luxury; a few, of more refined Senfations,
feek for it in Study and Retirement; while thofe
of more active Difpofitions look for in the bufy
World and amidft the Amufements of Society.
In vain does each flatter himfelf with the pleafing Hope of one Day enjoying the End of his
laborious Purfuit. ---- True Happinefs is feated
in the Mind, from whence alone proceed all the
Joys and Sorrows that checker human Life.
The Man who follows the Dictates of Reafon
and Confcience in a virtuous Courfe of Actions,
unaffaulted by the Stings of Guilt and Remorfe,
contented and refigned to the Will of Heaven,
whatfoever be his outward Condition, enjoys the
greateft Share of Felicity this World can beftow. Solon, one of the wife Men of Greece,
being afked by Cræsus, the wealthy King of
Lydia, who in the whole World was happier
than himfelf? anfwered " Tellus, who tho' he
" was poor, was a good Man, and content with
" what he had." And the great Philofopher
Socrates fays, that " Contentment is the
" Wealth of Nature, for it gives every thing
" we want, and really ftand in need of." The

Opinions

Opinions of many more of the antient heathen Sages might be produced in Supprt of this Argument; but these, I presume, will be sufficient, if we add to their Testimony that of a Christian and one of our own Countrymen, I mean Mr. ADDISON, who may truly be said to speak from Experience, when he says, that " a " good Conscience is to the Soul what Health is " to the Body ; it preserves a constant Ease and " Serenity within us, and more than countervails " all the Calamities and Afflictions that can " possibly befal us." But to drop Quotations, let me ask, who is more likely to obtain the truest Felicity than he whose sole Dependence is on the inexhaustible Fountain of Happiness ? In the comfortable Assurance of divine Favour, and in his exalted Hopes of Eternity, he looks with Contempt on the trivial Misfortunes and Difficulties of this Life, and at the same Time finds a double Relish in the innocent Enjoyments of it, because he is freed from all anxious Cares about Futurity.--- To paint the Deformity of Vice, and the transcendent Beauty of Virtue; to describe the many Inconveniencies incident to the one, and the Pleasure arising from the Exercise of the other, would better become a Pulpit than this Place, and be more fully illustrated by a set Discourse, than by my loose and scatter'd Reflections ; suffice it to say, that from the sensible Remarks of all the Gentlemen who have

H 2

spoken

spoken, I am fully convinced that a chearful
Serenity of Mind, which conftitutes the greateft
Part of fublunary Blifs, is not confined to any
outward Rank or Circumftances, but is equally
attainable by all, fince the only Sources from
whence it flows is a good Confcience, and a
contented Refignation to the Divine Will.

March 1ft, 1776.

———

QUESTION II. " Whether the placing of Vice
in a ferious or a ridiculous Light, is the better Way of reforming the Morals of Mankind ? "

Mr. Prefident,

"NOthing is more ridiculous than to be
" ferious about Trifles, and trifling
" about ferious Matters." This excellent Re-
mark I take the Liberty to quote from an ano-
nymous Author, as a Text or Prelude to my
Argument. The latter Part of it feems very
nearly to concern the prefent Queftion ; for what
is of a more ferious Nature than Vice ? which is
attended with the moft dreadful Confequences
to its Followers ; and yet, if treated in a jocofe
Manner, is liable to be confidered as lefs perni-
cious than it really is. Though, Mr. Prefident,
I would not willingly be ranked among thofe
flaming

flaming Zealots who continually thunder out
Damnation, Death and Deftruction againſt all
thoſe who do not embrace their fallible Opinions, yet, I muſt confeſs my Sentiments are
widely different from *theirs* alſo, who, by witty
Speeches would pretend to laugh Vice out of
Countenance. Perhaps in ſome leſs weighty
Matters, ſuch as a ridiculous Affectation, an o-
ver Preciſeneſs, a conceited Opinion of our Abi-
lities, and other Foibles (which can ſcarce be
rated as Vices) a pleaſant Raillery may ſome-
times have a very good Effect; but who, let
me aſk, ever ſaw the Profligate and Vicious reform'd by ſuch Means? or when did ever the
Repreſentation of a comic Piece convert a Knave
to an honeſt Man? I muſt own for my Part, I
never ſaw, read, or heard of ſuch an Inſtance.
Though I would by no Means be underſtood
wholly to condemn the rational Amuſement of
the Stage, yet I believe the comic Muſe, in general, has but little Pretenſions to Morality.
Health, Reputation, and our eternal Welfare
are Matters of too much Importance to be tri-
fled with, and the Loſs of them we can never
be too ſeriouſly and earneſtly warned againſt.
Sir Roger L'Eſtrange ſays, " the Fear of Hell
" does a great deal towards keeping us in the
" Way to Heaven; and if it were not for the Pe-
" nalty, the Laws neither of God nor of Man
" would be obeyed." To the Opinion of this
excellent

excellent Moralist I join my unfeigned Assent, and sincerely believe that a few serious moral Arguments deduced from the Consideration of a future State, such I mean as adorned the Writings of Addison, Tillotson, and Sherlock, have contributed, and will contribute more to the Advantage of Mankind, and the Reformation of Sinners, than all the Comedies, Jests, Lampoons, and Satires that ever made their Appearance in the World.

QUESTION III. " Whether the Passion of *Hope* " or *Fear* is the most predominant in the hu- " man Breast? "

Mr. President,

THE two opposite Passions Hope and Fear are, I believe, generally allowed to be the main Springs of all our Actions. Each of them its Turn operates more or less upon every Mind, and is the chief Cause of our Happiness and Misery in this Life. No one is so much oppressed with Misfortunes but has some Glimmerings of Hope, some agreeable Expectations of Futurity which comfort and support him; nor is any one so elevated with Prosperity, but that the Fears of what *may* happen, at certain Times discompose and terrify him. Yet if I may be allowed, from the little Knowledge I have had

of

of the human Heart, to deliver my Opinion
which of these two is most predominant, I must
give it in favour of Hope; for if our Fears
were so great as to overbalance our pleasing Expectations, added to the many Misfortunes Mankind is daily subject to, our Life must certainly
be insupportable; but that this is not the Case,
Experience evidently shews us; for where there
is one whom a continual Series of Troubles has
rendered desperate, I believe there are fifty to
be found who bravely surmount the greatest Difficulties, and if they do not immediately arrive
to the Fruition of their Hopes, continually look
forward, and flatter themselves with the agreeable, though uncertain Prospect of Futurity.
" When Faith, Temperance, the Graces, and
" other celestial Powers left the Earth (says one
of the Antients) " Hope was the only Goddess
" that staid behind." And the great Philoso-
pher Rochfoucault says, that " Hope is the last
" Thing that dies in Man; and tho' it be ex-
" ceedingly deceitful, yet it is of this great Use
" to us, that whilst we are travelling thro' Life,
" it conducts us an easier and more pleasant
" Way to our Journey's End."--- The ambitious Man flatters himself with the Prospect of future Honours, and overlooks all Dangers and
Impediments. The covetous Man hopes one
Day to enjoy the Benefit of his accumulated
Stores, not considering how soon Death may de-

prive

prive him of them. The Senfualift ftill hopes for the Enjoyment of *that* which he has yet never been able to obtain, viz. *real* Pleafure. While the good Man's Hopes are fixed on that delightful Object which he will one Day certainly enjoy in its utmoft Extent, a never-ceafing Flow of Happinefs, which will fatisfy the moft longing Defires of his Soul. This comfortable Profpect makes him foar above the fhort and trivial Inconveniences of this Life; vanquifhes every Fear that would affault his Peace, and daily convinces him of the immenfe Goodnefs and Wifdom of his Creator. --- This laft Inftance alone I think fufficiently proves the Falfhood of Mr. Hobbes's Doctrine, " that " Fear is the moft prevalent Paffion in the " human Breaft."

QUESTION IV. " Whether the Art of Poetry " or Oratory tends moft to the Promotion of " Virtue ? "

Mr. Prefident,

THE Promotion of Virtue, and Refinement of the Morals of Mankind ought to be the chief Bufinefs of every literary Science, as the mechanick Arts are principally defigned to affift the corporeal Faculties. Poetry and Oratory are both well qualified for the Purpofes of inculcating Religion and Goodnefs, as well as
eradicating

（ 59 ）

eradicating Vice and Infidelity. To such the immortal Strains of Milton, and the soft Numbers of Thomson are excellently adapted; nor less the solid Reasonings of Lock and Addison, and the pious Persuasions of Tillotson and Sherlock. Though at first it appears difficult to determine which of these two Sciences claims the Preference for their Merits in this respect, yet, on Examination, we must be compelled by its superior Efficacy to bestow the Laurels on Oratory. Moved by the gentle Admonitions that flow from the Lips of heavenly Eloquence, the Niggard is made liberal, the Prodigal parsimonious, the Libertine chaste, and the Epicurean temperate; while even the Atheist and Infidel are struck by its invincible Arguments, and taught the Necessity as well as Probability of a superintending Providence and future State. The same happy Effects, my Antagonists may argue, proceed also from Poetry; but these I answer are confined only to a few Persons of more refined Understandings, who are capable of relishing its sublime Beauties; the major Part of Mankind are wholly insensible to its Charms, and would esteem the successive Jinglings of Rhime and the regular Harmony of Measure no more than as an excellent *Opiate*. Those lofty Expressions which every where abound in real Poetry are as unintelligible to them as a foreign

I ·   Language.

Language. But Oratory, the more eafy and comprehenfive it is, the more excellent and forcible it appears both to the learned and the ignorant, and by addreffing the Paffions, as well as convincing the Reafon of Mankind, it muft certainly conduce more to the Promotion of Virtue than Poetry, which is generally calculated for the fublimer Feelings of Learning and Genius. Befides, when we are confined to Rhyme and Meafure we cannot be fuppofed to reafon with that Perfpicuity, nor even with that Energy which an important Subject requires. Were our Learned Advocates obliged to defend the Caufe of their Clients in·Verfe, their Pleadings would have but little Force in fupporting oppreffed Innocence; or were our Pulpit Orators obliged to chant forth the Denunciations of Heaven againft Vice and Irreligion in Rhyme and Meafure, their Difcourfes, for the moft Part, would be as much regarded by their Auditors as Sternhold & Hopkins's Verfion of the Pfalms. I muft therefore, Mr. Prefident, give my humble Opinion in favour of Eloquence.

A

A PASTORAL,

To the Memory of my worthy and much esteemed
Friend, Mr. DANIEL FOOT, late of Chichester,
who departed this Life the 26th of October,
1777.

THYRSIS *and* CORYDON.

THYRSIS.

WHILE all the plain a mournful prospect shews,
    And every breast with genuine sorrow glows ;
Whilst Damon's death the meads and groves bewail,
Why stand we here, nor join the plaintive tale ?

CORYDON.

Beneath yon antique grotto, brown with shade,
Where ivy boughs their circling foliage spread,
With hazels thick entwin'd, where elms display
Their spreading branches, and exclude the day ;
A gloomy scene, well suited to our care !
To sing his death, my Thyrsis, we'll repair :
Securely here may browze the bleating dams,
And Tityrus himself shall tend the lambs.

THYRSIS.

Since all around an awful silence reigns,
Begin, young Corydon, the plaintive strains.
Not softer music greets the blooming spring,
Nor swans expiring can so sweetly sing ;
Nor charms like you the mournful Philomel,
And Damon only could thy notes excel :
But since cold death has snatch'd him from our plains,
'Tis Corydon alone unrivall'd reigns.
Begin then, swain, the weeping numbers raise,
And every grove shall hearken to thy lays.

CORYDON.

Hear, Nature, hear, the mighty loss deplore,
Damon, the good, the virtuous, is no more !
Ye pow'rs auspicious, that delight to stray
Where Lavant leads his silver-winding way ;
Arcadian Pan, and all ye Sylvan train ;
Great Phœbus too, that loves the peaceful plain ;
Ye nymphs and shepherds, wreaths of cypress bring,
And ev'ry flow'r that decks the purple spring ;

Join

Join all the song, the mighty loss deplore,
Damon, the good, the virtuous, is no more!
Ye Muses, wail your darling son sincere,
And o'er his ashes shed the tender tear;
Lend all your aid, attune the golden lyre,
With softest strains my aching breast inspire;
With strains like those the hapless Damon sung,
When crowding sylvans listen'd to his tongue;
When good Philander ' was the woeful theme,
And hills and dales re-echoed to his name;
Then streams shall listen as I strike the shell,
And every breeze his hapless story tell,
Till Damon's name resound from shore to shore,
And forests sigh, The shepherd is no more!
Ye tuneful tenants of the drooping grove,
In silence sit, nor pour the strain of love;
Or whilst the brooks in mournful cadence flow,
Join the soft notes of sadly pleasing woe.
Behold the flocks decline their pensive heads,
Forsake the plain, and seek the silent shades!
Well may ye mourn! for who, when ting'd with gold
The welkin flames, shall drive you to the fold?
Or who shall shield your tender young from harm,
When Sirius rages, or when howls the storm?
Come then, ye flocks, your mighty loss deplore,
Damon, that lov'd your younglings, is no more!
See, Nature fades, the flow'ry honors die,
And all things droop beneath th'inclement sky;
In sighing murmurs winds their sorrow show,
And heav'n relents in sympathetic woe;
Alas! how chang'd the russet field appears!
See streams o'erflow the meadows with their tears!
No more the voice of melody complains,
No more are heard the shepherds tuneful strains;
But all, in silence hush'd, their loss deplore,
Damon their joy, their wonder, now no more!
What form is that thro' yonder cloud I spy,
More beauteous far than beams the orient sky?
'Tis Damon's self, in radiant glories crown'd,
Supremely fair, with circling angels round.—
Blest spirit! from yon realms of endless day,
With pity, oft thy toiling friends survey,

* The late Mr. George Smith.

And oh! direct, whilft we admire thy truth,
And copy thee thro' all the maze of youth!
That we may too † the fhafts of death defy,
And calmly yield to fate, nor fear to die;
Teach us content, nor ftill thy lofs deplore,
Since thou fhalt reign, when time fhall be no more.

THYRSIS.

Now ceafe the verfe to facred friendfhip due;
For fee how thick defcends the noxious dew,
The fetting fun now gilds the mountains heads,
And Night o'er all her fhadowy mantle fpreads;
Old Hylax barks, the flocks demand the fold,
And thro' the hazles blows the wintry cold.

F.

† *This line is not imaginary, but a faint allufion to a noble
fact.—Mr. Foot faid to his father, when he took his final leave,
"It is the difpenfation of divine Providence, and I am fatisfied,
I am not afraid to face my Creator, tho' unworthy, and I hope
we fhall all meet again in a place of uninterrupted felicity and
joy."*

'Quis defiderio fit pudor, aut modus
Tam chari capitas!

AN ELEGY

On the much-lamented Death of Mr. D. FOOT,
Junr., whofe many amiable Virtues render it a
publick as well as private Lofs.

BURST forth ye Tears, the mournful Tribute pay,
To facred Friendfhip tune the plaintive Lay;
Let Old and Young attend the mournful Song,
And drink the Notes that tremble on my Tongue;
Let mourning Nature the fad Lofs deplore,
DAMON is dead, and Pleafure is no more.

Yet

Yet will he live whilst Memory shall raise
The well-earn'd Trophy to deserving Praise;
While in our Hearts the Love of Truth shall warm,
And the sweet Train of softer Virtues charm;
With winning Ease still dawning in his Mind,
Each Act was sweeten'd, and each Thought refin'd;
In Candour, Wit, and Modesty he shone;
The dear Companion, and the pious Son;
With heav'nly Ardour glow'd his youthful Mien,
And smiling Joy once danc'd in every Vein;
Let mourning Nature the sad Loss deplore,
DAMON is dead, and Pleasure is no more.

Sooner shall PHILOMEL, when stolen her Young,
Forget to mourn, and pour the tender Song,
Than Time shall wear his Image from my Mind,
And leave no Vestige of my Friend behind;
Alas! nor inward Pangs, nor fervent Pray'rs,
Nor all thy Friends, nor all thy Parents Tears,
Nor all thy Merit in Religion's Cause,
Could shield thy Life from Death's devouring Jaws;
To thee, my Friend, who did so late rehearse
* PHILANDER's Death in sadly pleasing Verse;
To thee the Muse now tunes her plaintive Lays,
And gives this mournful Tribute to thy Praise:
Let fading Nature the sad Loss deplore,
DAMON is dead, and Pleasure is no more.

And thou, O cruel Fate! O partial Doom,
To crop such Godlike Virtues in their Bloom!
From mortal View to snatch his precious Head,
And damp each rising Joy with DAMON dead;
Tho' hence transferr'd to heav'nly Seats sublime,
His Virtues flourish in a milder Clime.
Ye mournful Parents arm the melting Soul,
And subject Passion to its just Controul;
Nor think that Time shall circumscribe his Race,
Or the strong Records of his Worth efface.
Still shall he live when this terrestrial Ball
By Time's dire Hand shall into Ruins fall;
In higher Seats shall move, shall still possess
The full Effusion of immortal Bliss;
There perfect Joys shall spring in endless Store,
And DAMON reign, and Pleasure evermore.

H. S.

* The late Mr. GEORGE SMITH, of Chichester.

F I N I S.